# TAKE ME OUT TO THE YAKYU

by Aaron Meshon

ATHENEUM BOOKS FOR YOUNG READERS · NEW YORK · LONDON · TORONTO · SYDNEY · NEW DELHI

To my MVP, Ayako

ATHENEUM BOOKS FOR
YOUNG READERS • An imprint of Simon &
Schuster Children's Publishing Division • 1230 Avenue
of the Americas, New York, New York 10020 • Copyright
© 2013 by Aaron Meshon • All rights reserved, including the
right of reproduction in whole or in part in any form. • ATHENEUM
BOOKS FOR YOUNG READERS is a registered trademark of Simon & Schuster,
Inc. • Atheneum logo is a trademark of Simon & Schuster, Inc. •
For information about special discounts for bulk purchases, please
contact Simon & Schuster Special Sales at 1-866-506-1949 or
business@simonandschuster.com. • The Simon & Schuster Speakers Bureau
can bring authors to your live event. For more information or to book an
event, contact the Simon & Schuster Speakers Bureau at 1-866-248-3049
or visit our website at www.simonspeakers.com. • Book design by Ann Bobco
and Aaron Meshon • The text for this book is set in Key. • The illustrations for
this book are rendered in acrylic paint. • Manufactured in China • 1112 SCP •
First Edition • 10  9  8  7  6  5  4  3  2  1 • Library of Congress Cataloging-in-
Publication Data • Meshon, Aaron. • p. cm. • Summary: A little boy's grandfathers,
one in America and one in Japan, teach him about baseball and its rich
varying cultural traditions. • ISBN 978-1-4424-4177-4 (hardcover) •
ISBN  978-1-4424-4178-1  (eBook)  •  [1.  Baseball—Fiction.
2. Grandfathers—Fiction. 3. Racially mixed people—Fiction.
4. Japan—Fiction.]  I. Title. • PZ7.M5492Tak 2013•
[E]—dc23 • 2011050907

I love baseball . . .

in America . . .                          and in Japan.

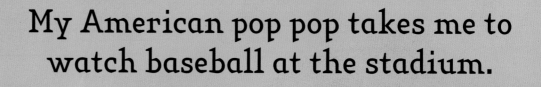

My American pop pop takes me to watch baseball at the stadium.

My Japanese ji ji takes me to
watch yakyu at the dome.

In America, we drive to the game in our long blue

In Japan, we ride

station wagon.

to the game in a short red bus that turns into a train.

In America, Pop Pop gets me a giant foam hand.

In Japan, Ji Ji gets me a giant plastic horn.

In America, Pop Pop also gets us hot dogs and peanuts before we find our seats.

In Japan, Ji Ji also gets us soba noodles and edamame before we find our seats.

In America,
the pitcher
throws
a 95-mile-
per-hour
**FASTBALL.**

In Japan,
the toushu
throws a
153-kilometer-
per-hour

SOKKYU.

In America, in the seventh inning,
we sing "Take Me Out to the Ball Game,"
and then we stretch!

In Japan, in the seventh inning,
we sing our team's anthem,
and then we let balloons go!

My favorite American team won!

My favorite Japanese team tied!

After the game, Pop Pop gets me my favorite player's jersey.

After the game, Ji Ji
gets me my favorite player's towel.

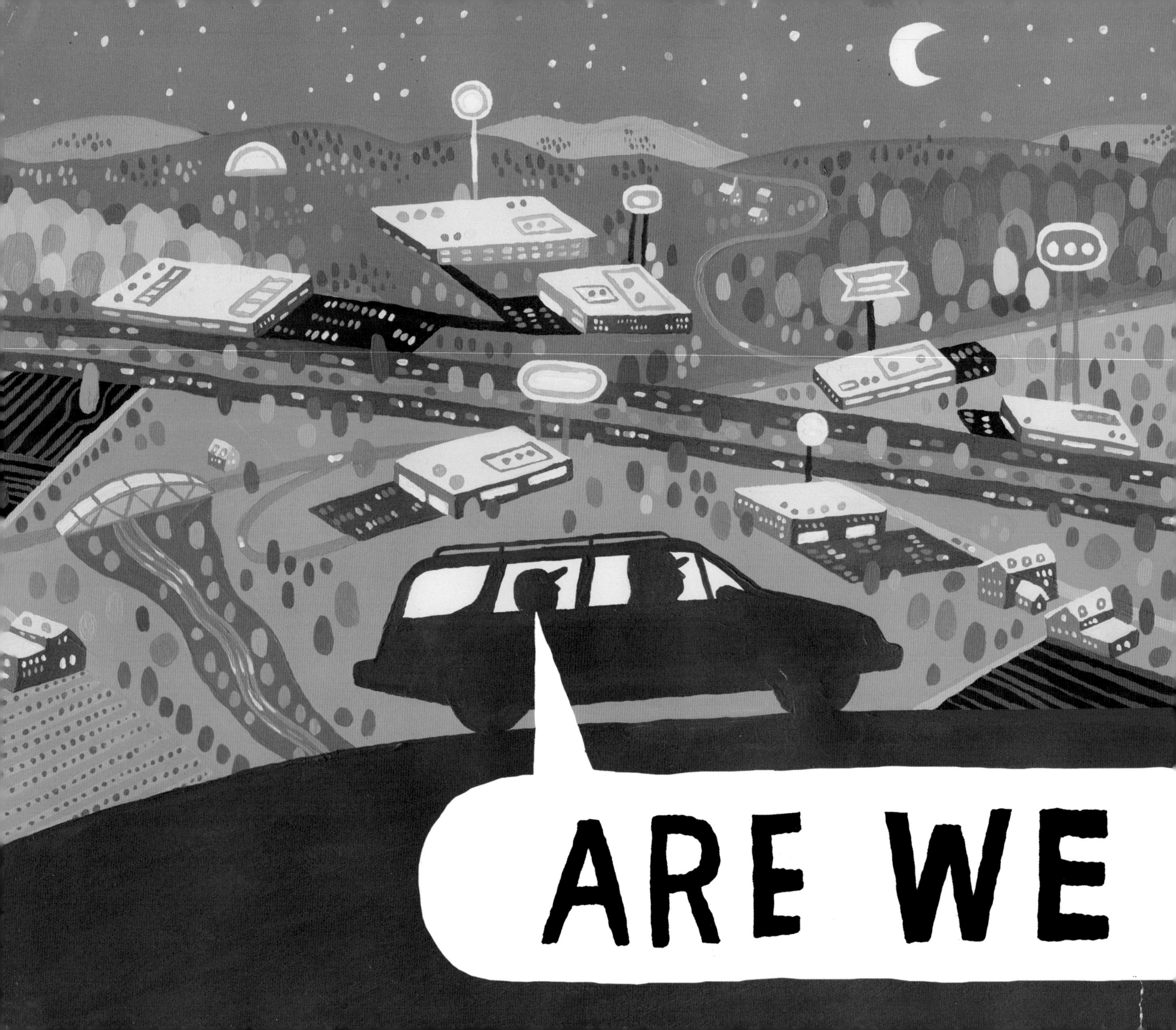
ARE WE

Gramma has a snack
and bath waiting for me.

Ba Ba has a snack
and ofuro waiting for me.

WHAT A WON

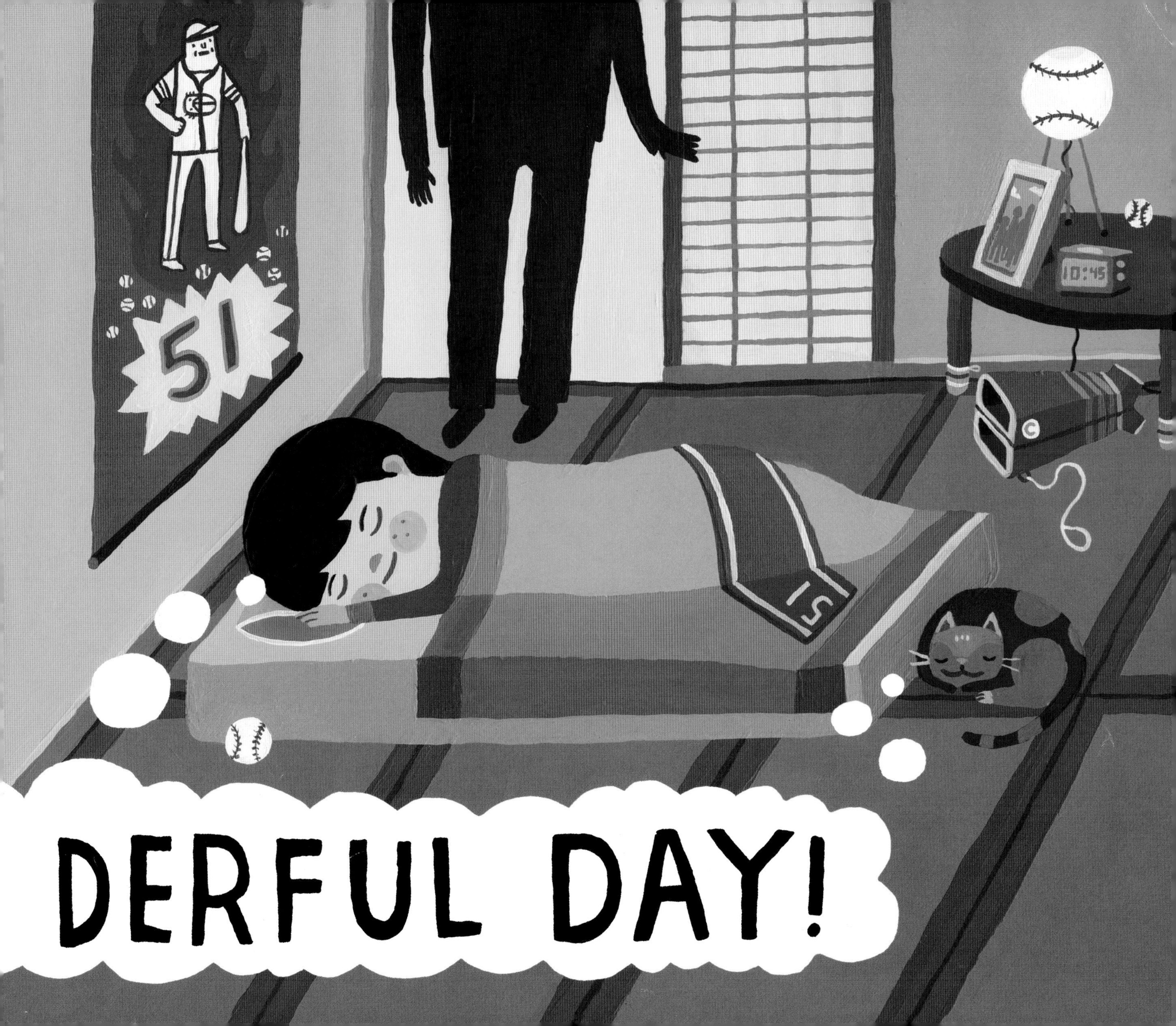
51
10:45
51
DERFUL DAY!

| Baseball | Yakyu やきゅう |
| Team | Chimu チーム |
| Pitcher | Toushu とうしゅ |
| Hitter | Dasha だしゃ |
| Home Run | Homuran ホームラン |
| Fastball | Sokkyu そっきゅう |
| Curveball | Kabu カーブ |
| Cheer | Ouen おうえん |
| Go for It | Ganbatte がんばって |

# Other Fun WORDS

| | |
|---|---|
| Grandfather/Pop Pop | Ojiichan/Ji Ji おじいちゃん／じいじ |
| Grandmom/Gramma | Obaachan/Ba Ba おばあちゃん／ばあば |
| Boy | Otokonoko おとこのこ |
| Bus | Basu バス |
| Train | Densha でんしゃ |
| Car | Kuruma くるま |
| Home | Uchi うち |
| Snack | Oyatsu おやつ |
| Bath | Ofuro おふろ |

# AUTHOR'S

### History of Baseball

Baseball is known as America's pastime. The first modern baseball game took place in Hoboken, New Jersey, in 1846. Many baseball teams and clubs were founded as baseball grew in popularity. Today there are dozens of professional teams and hundreds of minor league teams and recreational teams to root for! My first trip (in a long blue station wagon) to an American baseball stadium was in 1980 to watch the Philadelphia Phillies!

Baseball is one of the most watched sports in Japan. Baseball was introduced to Japan in 1872 and quickly became very popular. There are many teams in Japan to cheer for, and even high school baseball is extremely popular. The whole country watches the live high school tournaments in spring and summer. My first trip (in a short red bus that turned into a train) to a Japanese baseball dome was in 2005 to watch the Nagoya Dragons!

### Game Length

In America most baseball games last for nine innings, but if both teams are tied when the ninth inning ends, the teams continue playing until one team has the lead at the end of the played inning. The most innings of any modern American baseball game is twenty-six innings (you could eat a lot of hot dogs in that time!). American baseball games do not end in ties.

# NOTE

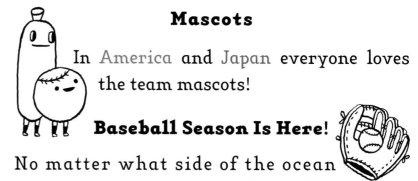

In Japan baseball games are played for nine innings. If both teams are tied when the ninth inning ends, they continue playing until one team has the lead at the end of the played inning, but only to the twelfth inning. If the teams are still tied in the twelfth inning, then the game ends in a tie. Japanese trains don't run after midnight (and it gets too late for bath time!).

## Stadiums and Domes

In America most baseball games are played in open-air stadiums. It is great because you can see the summer sky, but if it rains a lot and the field gets too wet, the games are sometimes canceled. There are a few domes in America, and they protect the fans and players from the summer heat and the late-spring chill.

In Japan most baseball games are played inside air-conditioned domes. They protect the fans and players from the superhot and humid summers.

## Mascots

In America and Japan everyone loves the team mascots!

## Baseball Season Is Here!

No matter what side of the ocean I am on, I can't wait for baseball season to start so I can watch my favorite teams and be with my family. I love baseball and my family!